RABBIT SURPRISE

RABBIT SURPRISE

by Eric L. Houck, Jr.

illustrated by
Dominic Catalano

CROWN PUBLISHERS, INC.
New York

For Brenda and Jennifer
—E. L. H., Jr.

To Tracy Gates—Thank you for believing in me.
—D. C.

Published by Crown Publishers, Inc., a Random House company, 225 Park Avenue South, New York, New York 10003.

CROWN is a trademark of Crown Publishers, Inc.

Manufactured in Hong Kong

Library of Congress Cataloging-in-Publication Data

Houck, Eric L., 1961–
    Rabbit surprise / by Eric L. Houck, Jr. ; illustrated by Dominic Catalano.
       p.   cm.
    Summary: Richard Fox must rely on a trick of his own when a magic hat left at his door produces more and more rabbits.
    [1. Magic—Fiction.   2. Foxes—Fiction.   3. Rabbits—Fiction.]
I. Catalano, Dominic, ill.   II. Title.
PZ7.H81144Rab   1993
[E]—dc20   92-1318
ISBN 0-517-58777-7 (trade)
       0-517-58778-5 (lib. bdg.)

10 9 8 7 6 5 4 3 2 1   First Edition

Richard Fox crawled
out of bed to answer a
knock at the door.

There was a picnic
basket on the front step.
The note on it read—
A breakfast treat just for you.
Love,
Grandmother Fox
Richard brought the
basket in and set it on the
table in the kitchen. He
carefully lifted the lid.
One, two, three, four. Four
little rabbits popped up.
In the basket with the
rabbits was a
magician's black hat.

"How clever," he thought. "Four little rabbits for breakfast and a magic-hat centerpiece for the table."

Richard put a bouquet of flowers in the hat. Then he went to get a frying pan.

When he came back,
the flowers had vanished.
Four little rabbits sat on
the table.

One, two, three, four.
Four *more* little rabbits
peeked out of the hat.

"Incredible!" Richard
said. He went to get a
larger pan.

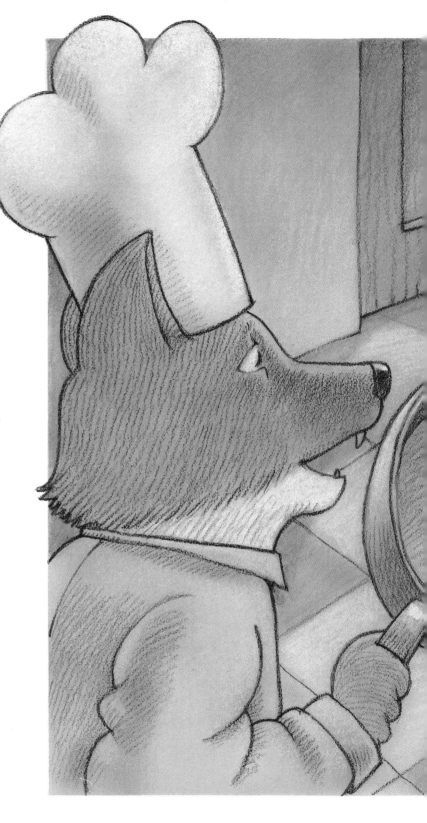

When he came back,
there were *eight* little
rabbits on the table.

One, two, three, four.
Four *more* little rabbits
peeked out of the hat.

Richard dropped his
pans. "I can't eat all these
rabbits," he said.

He went to the
telephone and called his
brother, Johnny Fox.

When he came back, there were *twelve* little rabbits, and the table was overflowing.

Four *more* little rabbits peeked out of the hat. Now there were more rabbits than Richard could count.

Little rabbits started hopping out of the hat, one right after another. They were climbing in the cupboards, swimming in the sink, fiddling with the toaster. . . .

Just then there was a knock at the door.

It was Johnny.

"Quick!" Richard said. "There are thousands of little rabbits all over my kitchen."

Johnny looked around. "And on your couch," he said. "And on the TV, the stereo, and down the hall...."

There were little rabbits everywhere.

"We've got to get rid of that hat," Richard said. They pushed their way into the kitchen.

A BIG rabbit was climbing out of the hat. He carried a magic wand.

"Salutations!" he said. "And welcome to the show." He waved his wand. Carrots appeared from thin air and showered to the floor.

"Carrots for everyone!" he shouted. The little rabbits cheered.

"For my next trick I will levitate an audience volunteer." He waved his wand.

Johnny floated up. "Ouch!" he cried, hitting his head on the ceiling. The little rabbits thumped their applause.

"And now I will pull a rabbit out of my hat."

"No!" Richard yelled. "No more rabbits!"

"Boooo," cried the little rabbits. The big rabbit frowned at Richard. Then he grinned.

"Okay," he said. "For my next trick I will saw *you* in half." The little rabbits cheered wildly.

"Hey! You can't do *that*, either!"

"Yes, yes, yes," chanted the little rabbits.

"I am a *great* magician," the big rabbit said. "I can do anything."

Richard's eyes lit up. "*Anything?*"

"Anything at all," the big rabbit replied.

"I bet you can't make things disappear."

"Piece of cake," the big rabbit said.

He snapped his fingers, and the cake on the counter disappeared.

Richard raised his eyebrows. "Not bad," he said, "but how about something harder, like...that hat?"

"Yes! Yes! Do it! Do it!" squealed the little rabbits.

"Easy as pie," the big rabbit said, and he waved his wand.

POOF

POOF! The hat disappeared in a puff of smoke.

"Uh-oh," the big rabbit said, and he disappeared too.

"Uh-oh," the little rabbits said.

Four, three, two, one. Four, three, two, one. Little rabbits began disappearing all over the place.

Johnny fell from the ceiling. *"Oof."* He landed on Richard.

When they got up, all the rabbits were gone.

"Wow," Richard said. "That was close. But now there's nothing for breakfast."

"You can come home with me," Johnny invited. "Grandma Fox left a big basket by my door this morning."

"There should be more than enough for two...."